MASTERS OF DISASTERS

THE EARTHSHAKING
EARTHQUAKE
MYSTERY

D1482586

By
Carole Marsh

Published by Gallopade International/Carole Marsh Books. Printed in the United States of America.

Managing Editor: Sherry Moss
Senior Editor: Janice Baker
Assistant Editor: Chris Roosen
Cover Design & Illustrations: John Kovaleski (www.kovaleski.com)
Content Design: Darryl Lilly, Outreach Graphics

Gallopade International is introducing SAT words that kids need to know in each new book that we publish. The SAT words are bold in the story. Look for this special logo beside each word in the glossary. Happy Learning!

Gallopade is proud to be a member and supporter of these educational organizations and associations:

American Booksellers Association
International Reading Association
National Association for Gifted Children
The National School Supply and Equipment Association
The National Council for the Social Studies
Museum Store Association
Association of Partners for Public Lands

This book is a complete work of fiction. This book makes reference to Universal Studios Hollywood. This book is not authorized or endorsed by Universal Studios, Inc. or any other businesses named in the book. All attractions, product names, or other works mentioned in this book are trademarks of their respective owners and the names and images used in this book are strictly for editorial purposes; no commercial claims to their use is claimed by the author or publisher.

20 YEARS AGO . . .

As a mother and an author, one of the fondest periods of my life was when I decided to write mystery books for children. At this time (1979) kids were pretty much glued to the TV, something parents and teachers complained about the way they do about web surfing and blogging today.

I decided to set each mystery in a real place—a place kids could go and visit for themselves after reading the book. And I also used real children as characters. Usually a couple of my own children served as characters, and I had no trouble recruiting kids from the book's location to also be characters.

Also, I wanted all the kids—boys and girls of all ages—to participate in solving the mystery. And, I wanted kids to learn something as they read. Something about the history of the location. And I wanted the stories to be funny. That formula of real+scary+smart+fun served me well.

I love getting letters from teachers and parents who say they read the book with their class or child, then visited the historic site and saw all the places in the mystery for themselves. What's so great about that? What's great is that you and your children have an experience that bonds you together forever. Something you shared. Something you both cared about at the time. Something that crossed all age levels—a good story, a good scare, a good laugh!

20 years later,
Carole Marsh

Hey, kids! As you see, here we are ready to embark on another of our exciting Carole Marsh Mystery adventures. My grandchildren often travel with me all over the world as I research new books. We have a great time together, and learn things we will carry with us for the rest of our lives!

I hope you will go to www.carolemarshmysteries.com and explore the many Carole Marsh Mysteries series!

Well, the Mystery Girl is all tuned up and ready for "take-off!" Gotta go...Papa says so! Wonder what I've forgotten this time?

Happy "Armchair Travel" Reading,

Mimi

ABOUT THE CHARACTERS

Artemis Masters is an absentminded genius. He's a scientist at the top of his field in the early detection of natural disasters. Everyone looks to him to solve the mysteries of nature...he just needs someone to find his car keys, shoes and glasses!

Curie Masters, though only 12, has inherited her father's intelligence and ability to see things others don't. She has a natural penchant to solve mysteries...even if it means tangling with those older and supposedly smarter than her.

Nick Masters, an 8-year-old boy who's tall enough to pass as 12, likes to match wits with his sister and has her desire to solve mysteries others overlook. While he's the younger sibling, he tends to want to protect his sister, and of course, be the first to solve the mystery.

BOOKS IN THIS SERIES:

#1 The Earthshaking Earthquake Mystery

#2 The Treacherous Tornado Mystery

#3 The Horrendous Hurricane Mystery

TABLE OF CONTENTS

1   Gentlemen, Start Your Engines 1

2   Two Wrongs Don't Make a Right,
They Make A Left 13

3   Nobody's Asphalt But Mine 21

4   Blanket Coverage 35

5   Tremors 39

6   A Whole Lotta Shaking Going On 45

7   Wipe Your Feet Before You Take Your Seat 57

8   Getting There is Half the Fun, Sort Of 61

9   Here, There...Uh, Nowhere! 65

10   Rolling Through No Man's Land 73

11   There She Blows! 81

12   Pedal To The Meddle 91

13   I Scream, You Scream, We All Scream
For the Home Team 93

14   If It is Not One Thing, It is Definitely the Other . .99

15   Is That A Rumble, Or Did Your
Tummy Grumble? 105

About the Author 111

Book Club Talk About It! 112

Book Club Bring It To Life! 113

Earthshaking Earthquake Trivia 114

Glossary 116

Tech Connects 118

CHAPTER ONE:

GENTLEMEN, START YOUR ENGINES

      It's a space ship...no, it's a van...well, maybe it's a little bit of both. Alien-looking with its numerous antennae sticking out every which way, like a Mars lunar lander, the van sat on a perilous angle in front of the Masters' home. It teetered on a block wedged under the back tire that kept it from rolling down the steep San Francisco street, through Mrs. Potters' garden, past the grocery store, and into the Pacific Ocean. The black tires, thick with mud, could tell as many stories as the bumper stickers plastered on the once shiny metal bumper. A blazing orange bumper sticker stuck in the middle of Oklahoma and Nebraska reads: CAUTION: I BRAKE FOR DISASTERS!

Inside the house was a storm of seismic proportions. Gadgets upon gadgets littered the living room floor. Several television sets lined the far wall where 24-hour news and weather reports from all over the world chattered away. Stuck in the middle of the chaos was Dr. Artemis Masters. He looked exactly how you'd expect a somewhat-mad scientist to look. His hair poked out everywhere like he'd just stuck his finger in an electrical socket. Eyeglasses were perched on his nose; another set dangled from a chain around his neck, and then there was that lab coat that was two sizes too big.

While anyone else would be distracted by the unnerving jibber-jabber of countless languages around him, Artemis focused on the task at hand. He was figuring out a series of random numbers that made Einstein's Theory of Relativity seem like basic arithmetic.

Downstairs, in a room oddly neat compared to the rest of the house, Copernicus Masters, tall for an 8-year-old, fiddled with a computer game controller. His sister Curie, 11, thumbed through a science book almost as big as she was. Their unique names were to be expected. Their father knew from the moment they were born that they would both be famous scientists, just like him. Copernicus, also known as Nick, was named after Nicholas Copernicus, the first person to propose that the sun is the center of the universe. Curie got her name from Marie Curie, famous for her work on radioactivity, and a two-time Nobel Prize winner.

Like most kids, they liked to eat chocolate, would rather do anything other than pick up their rooms, enjoyed video games and the park. They just happened to have a genius IQ, and the ability to see things in ways most people don't—adults included. And like most siblings, they were competitive, each hoping to stay one step ahead of the other.

"I just love summer vacation," said Nick, as he focused on the television. "I'm not going to do anything but sit back and play video games."

Next to him, Curie curled up with the anchor-sized book on the solar system, ready to read. "Well, I'm going to use my time wisely and catch up on all my pleasure reading," Curie said.

Challenged, Nick sneaked a peek at the book. "I've already read it," he said. "Twice."

"Then what's it about, *Copernicus*?" Curie smirked as she covered up the title.

"It's, uhm, the theory, of...no wait, the study of...." Nick wasn't doing so well in his video game anymore as he tried to weave a convincing tale. Suddenly, he saw a reflection of the book's title in the television screen.

"You don't know, do you?" Curie smiled.

"Sure I do. It's an encyclopedia of the solar system," said Nick.

Curie couldn't believe her ears. "How did you know that? I just checked this book out of the library," she said. But before Nick could answer, a red light flashed and a loud horn honked like a sick goose.

"Another one of Dad's practice runs. Come on, let's go," said Nick, popping up quickly.

Curie followed her brother up the stairs. "I'll figure out how you knew the book title," she warned.

Artemis' eyes were wider than the Grand Canyon as he watched the numbers on his computer screen come together in a pattern known only to him. Nick and Curie walked into the room, unconcerned, as they had done a thousand times before.

"Come on, Dad, safety positions!" said Nick, but Artemis didn't move. His eyes were glued to the computer screen, and he heard nothing but the whirring of gears between his ears.

"I finally did it, kids. I've unraveled the secrets behind tectonic plates! Your dad is one step away from winning the Nobel Prize! *The Nobel Prize!*" Artemis cried. Both Nick and Curie stopped in their tracks. This was not what they expected.

"Do you know what this means?" asked Curie.

"He figured out how to track earthquakes?" said Nick.

"Then this isn't a practice run!" said Curie.

Suddenly afraid, they both dashed to different parts of the room—Nick to the doorway and Curie under a large table with elephant trunk legs.

"What about Dad?" asked Curie. They both looked at their father, gazing at the computer screen, lost in his own world.

"Come on, Dad!" shouted Nick. He looked like he wanted to leave his protective area under the doorway and pull his dad to safety. Curie had the same idea, and she planned to beat her brother to it. They ran to Artemis at the same time, both hoping to save him before the roof came crashing down around them all! Nick grabbed one arm, Curie the other, and a game of tug of war began.

"Curie," said Nick. "Let go!"

"Nick, you know that being under a large table is safer than being in a doorway," Curie lectured, like an older sister.

"Now is not the time to drop 100 IQ points," said Nick. "The doorway has always been the best place, so please let go of Dad's arm and follow me."

"Table!" shouted Curie.

"Doorway!" cried Nick.

The two ping-ponged back and forth, with Artemis stuck in the middle. But instead of being torn between the two, his eyes remained glued to his computer screen where the random number formula ticked down, down, down.

"Here it comes!" said Artemis, like a boy awaiting the ice cream truck. Nick and Curie studied the computer screen, which seemed like a digital countdown to doomsday. Forgetting about who was right or wrong, they decided to **abort** their plan. They both let go of Artemis, and quickly crossed over each other as they headed to the other's safety zone. Nick cowered under the table while Curie braced herself in the doorway, both waiting for the impending roller coaster ride that is an **EARTHQUAKE**.

And they waited.

And waited.

But nothing happened.

"Did you feel it?" said Artemis, beaming. Both Curie and Nick looked at their dad as if he was just a little crazier than he appeared.

"Dad, nothing happened," said Curie, slightly confused.

"Maybe it's just a delayed reaction?" Nick said from under the table. But Curie didn't wait to find out. She hurried over to her father and double-checked his calculations.

"Are you sure you programmed the computer correctly?" asked Curie. "Took all the variables into consideration?"

Not wanting his sister to have the upper hand, Nick dashed to her side. "There's nothing wrong. I checked his calculations myself, Curie," he said.

"Like I said, Dad, did you make sure it was programmed correctly?" said Curie.

"That's not funny," said Nick with a frown.

"No, no, all the calculations are correct, see," said Artemis. He pointed to another display monitor where a digital Richter scale was displayed. A tiny blip barely stood out on the flat lines. "This data here, the one before the marker," said Artemis.

"You mean the blip?" said Nick.

"It's a marker, Nick, and before that marker, these orange lines predicted this earthquake!" said Artemis, pointing to the tiny blip.

"That could be a car backfiring, Dad," said Curie. It was her turn to frown, as she knew that the tiny movement could be anything at all.

"Or a random occurrence explained away by a series of incorrect data," said Nick.

"Or it means that my Earthquake Early Warning Detection Device really works!" said Artemis.

He fumbled with his paperwork stacked together like a pile of chicken feathers. He grabbed all his papers and hurried out of the room.

Nick and Curie studied the data and readouts left behind.

"What do you think, Nick?" asked Curie.

"He could be on to something," said Nick.

"Do you really think so?" asked Curie.

"Just because you said there could be a correlation to a car backfiring doesn't mean it's improbable," said Nick.

"Improbable? It's preposterous!" said Curie.

Nick felt he should break it down in simple terms for his older sister. "Curie, pressure is put on the earth's crust like this," he said. He brought the sides of his hands together.

"I know, Nick. The first layer, which is the crust, is broken into tectonic plates which rub up against each other," said Curie.

"Yes, Curie, but you never know when that friction is going to create enough stress to cause an earthquake," said Nick. He brought his words into action, rubbing his hands harder and faster, until his own tectonic plates ruptured, creating a mini-disaster by knocking over a cup of water on the desk.

"Oh, no!" said Nick. Both kids pushed and pulled papers out of the water's path. Nick suddenly kicked off his shoes and yanked off his socks.

"You're not going to stop it by stinking it out," said Curie, as she held her nose.

"Ha-ha, Curie," said Nick, as he wiped up the water with his dirty socks. "You could help me, you know."

"I'm not touching your stinky socks," said Curie.

"Then get some paper towels, please," said Nick.

Curie turned to grab them, but stopped when she saw her dad struggling with an oversized suitcase.

"I think paper towels will do, Dad," said Curie. Artemis looked around, puzzled.

"Okay, that's fine. We can take some paper towels, too," said Artemis, as he pulled the suitcase toward the door.

"Dad, what are you doing with that suitcase?" said Curie. Artemis looked at his daughter as if the answer was as plain as the nose on her face.

"Well, loading up the van, of course. We've got a job to do," said Artemis.

"But our summer vacation just started," said Curie. "And Bella, my best friend ever, is having a sleepover tonight, and they got a new puppy named Chase I wanted to play with! Look, she gave me this special electronic bracelet that says *Best Friends for Life*."

"No, no. No time for that. Copernicus, help me with this," said Artemis. Nick forgot about his wet socks and reached for the suitcase.

"Nick, what are you doing?" asked Curie.

"Getting ready for an adventure, silly," said Nick.

"But you said that all you wanted to do this summer was lie around and play video games," said Curie.

"If Dad has stumbled upon a great invention, I want to be a part of it," said Nick, as he and Artemis worked the suitcase out the door. Curie thought for a moment, and then hurried after them.

"Wait for me!" she called.

As Curie followed them out the door, red letters flashed across the computer screen: WARNING: MOVEMENT ALONG THE FAULT LINE!

CHAPTER TWO:

TWO WRONGS DON'T MAKE A RIGHT, THEY MAKE A LEFT

The van shook, rattled and rolled as if a wrestling match were going on inside. And the truth wasn't that far off. In the passenger's seat, Nick and Curie were locked in battle.

"I got here first!" said Nick.

"But I'm older!" said Curie, as she tried to squeeze into the "co-pilot" seat, where the lucky rider was responsible for monitoring the Global Positioning Satellite (GPS) Navigation system, and controlling the CD player. Nick pushed back, and then reached for the seat belt to buckle himself in.

Artemis studied a set of notes as he climbed into the van, unaware of the wrestling match next to

him. He checked the gauges that made the van look more like the cockpit of a commercial jet plane. Artemis was confused since they were not working. He tapped them, but nothing happened. He finally realized that something was missing.

"What did I do with my keys?" said Artemis. Both Nick and Curie pointed to the ignition where a rubber microscope dangled from a giant bundle of keys. "Oh, right. Thanks," said Artemis. He turned the key and the van coughed to life. "Okay, kids. Buckle up." Artemis finally saw the struggle next to him. "Hey, come on, kids. Only one in a seat."

"Dad, I was here first, and she's trying to push me out," said Nick.

"But I always get the front seat first, because I'm the oldest," said Curie.

"Well, now I'm taller than you, so I should get it," said Nick.

Artemis cleared his throat. Nick and Curie stopped and looked at their dad.

"We're wasting valuable time here while you two bicker over who is going to sit in Command-Com," said Artemis. "You both have brains and IQs equal to mine. Don't you think you can solve this situation responsibly?" said Artemis.

"Okay. Rock, paper, scissors," said Nick as he made a fist. Curie scoffed at his idea.

"How about this, Nick. We take turns. Since I am the oldest, I'll ride in Command-Com first, then after the first stop, you will," said Curie.

"But, what about," said Nick, but his protest was cut off by his father.

"That sounds fair to me, Nick," said Artemis.

Sulking, Nick slowly crawled into the backseat and buckled up. Artemis smiled at him in the rear-view mirror, and then turned to Curie.

"Pilot to co-pilot. All systems go?" said Artemis. Nick mouthed Curie's response, wishing he were the one up there.

"Roger that, captain. All systems are A-OK. Kick the tires and light the fires," said Curie, as she put on a pair of sunglasses. Artemis flipped his sunglasses down over his prescription lenses, gave a thumbs up, then put the van in gear. Curie turned and smiled confidently at Nick, who looked out the window.

"Let's see. Who should we listen to? How about the Venice Beach Girls?" said Curie. She reacted to Artemis, who cleared his throat again lightly. "Hey, Nick, who would you like to listen to?" asked Curie. Before Nick could answer, Artemis had pulled over to the curb and parked the van.

"Okay, we're here," said Artemis, as he flipped up his sunglasses and opened the door.

"We're where?" said Curie, confused.

"We've arrived at the first research point," said Artemis.

"But, Dad, we're less than a block from the house. We could have walked here," said Curie. Artemis laughed as if that was the funniest thing he had ever heard.

"And carry all the equipment?" said Artemis as he walked toward the back of the van. Nick, now happier than ever with the deal he made, smiled as he unbuckled his seat belt.

"Don't gloat, Copernicus," said Curie.

Both kids helped their dad unload boxes, computers, cables and other stuff from the back of the van.

"Why are we here, Dad? I mean, what's so important about downtown San Francisco?" asked Curie.

Artemis stopped and pretended to be in shock. "Are you sure you're my daughter?" he asked.

Suddenly, Curie got it. "The San Francisco earthquake of 1906!" she shouted.

"It was one of the worst natural disasters to hit the United States," said Artemis. "Experts estimated the earthquake to register 8.3 on the Moment Magnitude Scale. Much of what we see here was gone. This city was rebuilt almost from the ground up," he added.

"If it was such a bad earthquake, Dad, why did they rebuild it so close to the epicenter?" said Nick.

"Maybe they didn't know that the epicenter is the point on the earth's surface directly above where an earthquake originates? After all, it was more than one hundred years ago," said Curie, as she helped Artemis unpack his big black case.

"I think it's more of an emotional thing, Curie," Artemis replied. "The people who lived through the 1906 earthquake didn't want to give up what they built. Though the earthquake caused an estimated $500 million in damage, left almost 3,000 people dead and 300,000 homeless, it was important to them to reclaim a sense of normalcy."

"So, what are we going to do now? Stay here until the next big earthquake hits?"asked Nick.

"No, we're going to check out the line of Masters' Motion Sensors that I set up along the San Andreas Fault when I started this project," said Artemis.

"So that's what's sending back the information to the central computer set up in the van," said Nick.

"That's right son, and if my calculations are correct, it will be able to tell us when the next 'big one' will strike," said Artemis.

They walked to a planter where a shade tree sheltered a small mound of dirt. While Nick was proud of himself for being in tune with his dad, Curie was more interested in their surroundings. Something just wasn't right. She looked down at several candy wrappers that littered the ground. Ordinarily, this wouldn't be an odd thing in such a large city, but they all seemed to be in direct proximity to Artemis' invention.

"What's this?" asked Artemis. But it wasn't the candy wrappers that concerned him. It looked like someone had been digging around the planter. Artemis got down on his hands and knees to get a closer look, but quickly jumped to his feet. "Dog," he said as he rubbed his nose and let out a sneeze of seismic proportions.

The kids knew what that sneeze meant. Their father was allergic to dogs, which doomed any chance that they'd ever own one. But that's okay. They had adventures.

Artemis tried to control the super sneeze attack so he could get back to work, but they came quicker than firecrackers. He walked to the van and grabbed a handful of tissues.

Nick followed his dad, but Curie grabbed his collar.

"Hey, that hurt!" shouted Nick. He saw the look on his sister's face, and knew she wasn't trying to be mean. "What's the matter?" he asked. His eyes followed Curie's hand down to the pile of candy wrappers. "It wasn't a dog, was it?" he added.

"A dog was here, but he didn't eat those candy bars," said Curie.

Nick filtered the loose dirt through his fingers. "And he might not have dug up this dirt," he added.

The two studied the scene. It was obvious that someone was searching for something—quite possibly the Masters' Motion Sensors. Nick grabbed his laptop. With his fingers a blur, the Masters' Motion Sensor program popped onto the screen, followed by the words: WARNING: MOVEMENT ALONG THE FAULT LINE!

The kids looked at each other, wide-eyed.

"Well," said Curie, "that means that either Dad's invention works, or someone has been tampering with it!"

CHAPTER THREE:

NOBODY'S ASPHALT BUT MINE

The tires hummed across the asphalt as city turned to countryside, countryside to desert. A sign in the distance read: *Los Angeles, 17 Miles.*

Though he was planted in the Command-Com seat, sunglasses absorbing most of his face, Nick was unable to enjoy it. His mind whirred like a top, focused on the mystery. He looked back at his sister, and she too was trying to figure out if it was a coincidence, or if someone was **deliberately** messing with their father's work.

The van entered the city of Northridge, California, home to the 1994 Northridge earthquake that shook the city's foundation. Artemis kept driving until he came to a large dirt lot caged in by a tattered chain link fence. On either side were apartment buildings. Nick stretched as Artemis got out and walked toward the empty lot on a street filled with apartments and businesses. Before he could tell Curie that they had stopped, she opened his door.

"Did you come up with any ideas?" asked Curie.

"No. Did you?" her brother asked.

"Well, other than a dog with a sweet tooth, no," she said.

"It was probably just a coincidence," Nick tried to convince himself as he jumped from the van to follow his sister. But he had the mind of a master sleuth and couldn't help but notice a black car parked just down the street. It looked out of place in this neighborhood. He took a mental picture of it, and then ran after his sister.

"What are we doing here?" asked Curie.

"Well, to know for sure if my invention works, we need to place more Masters' Motion Sensors along the fault line," said Artemis, "and research leads me to believe that this is the epicenter of the 1994 Northridge earthquake."

"Was it the same as the San Francisco earthquake?" asked Nick.

"No, quite different. Which makes studying earthquakes so exciting," said Artemis with a big grin.

"And scary," added Nick.

"This earthquake occurred on a blind thrust fault, which is where the end of the fault, called a plane, ends before it reaches the surface," said Artemis.

"How can you find them if they don't reach the surface?" asked Curie.

"Well, you can't. Which is why I have been working on this invention," said Artemis. "And this earthquake produced the strongest ground motions ever recorded in North America. Damage was widespread. Major sections of freeways, parking garages and office buildings collapsed. And many apartment buildings were damaged beyond repair. Just like the one that used to stand here," added Artemis, spreading his arms out.

Artemis noticed the look of fear on Nick's face, and put his arm around his shoulder. "Don't be afraid, son," said Artemis. "I know that earthquakes can be scary, but each one we study teaches us how they work." Artemis pulled out his seismic measuring equipment. "What we learned about damage to buildings from other earthquakes allowed us to retrofit buildings and reduce the amount of destruction and lives lost," said Artemis.

"What is retrofitting, Dad?" asked Nick.

Before Artemis could answer, Curie did. "It means when a building is brought up to new standards so it will be able to handle the stress from an earthquake in the future," she said proudly.

"Very good," her dad replied, then suddenly stopped. The quirky things their father did usually didn't bother them, but this one was probably one of the strangest. Artemis put his arms out like a weather vane, taking **deliberate** steps to see where the best place was to put the Masters' Motion Sensors. "Knowing where the building was will help me determine how best to monitor the fault line," he said.

"With the building gone, I need to use my instincts to find the best place for it."

"Hang on, Dad. I think I can help," Nick said as he ran back to the van to grab his laptop. With the black sedan still on his mind, he grabbed a small computer circuit board out of the recycle bin, stuffed it in his pocket, and dashed back.

"What have we got there, Nick?" asked Artemis as his son powered up the laptop.

"I'm looking for a database of buildings either by satellite photo or some sort of collection of photographs," Nick said as his fingers flew across the keyboard. In no time at all, Nick pulled up a photograph of the city streets by satellite. "Here we go," he said. He brought the image in closer, getting better and better detail until the flowers in the window box on the apartment building were crystal clear.

"Wow! That's perfect, Nick. Don't get any closer," said Artemis. He studied the picture, and then looked at the empty lot. In his mind's eye, the building came to life. He looked at a readout in his hand that described the power of the earthquake.

Suddenly, the ground shook. Car alarms wailed and dogs barked. The flower box in the window dropped to the ground and shattered into a thousand pieces. The building tilted and groaned, then crumbled to its knees. Artemis' body seemed to move with the shaking and rolling. Nick and Curie watched with curiosity as their father relived the earthquake in his mind.

Then things went quiet; back to normal. Artemis had broken from his daydream and walked quickly toward a space almost exactly in the center of the empty lot.

"Looks like he found what he was looking for," said Curie. She and Nick followed their dad.

But Nick wasn't really listening. He was more concerned with a shiny new candy wrapper that just didn't fit with all the old trash. He quickly grabbed it as Artemis pointed to a grouping of lines that looked like mud that had dried and cracked under the hot sun.

"Do you see how this spider web of lines crisscross?" Artemis asked. "While they're not specifically fault lines, they give us a pretty good idea of just how complex the tectonic plates are."

"And they give us a great central point to put the Masters' Motion Sensor," said Curie. She turned over the soft dirt with a shovel. Artemis readied the Masters' Motion Sensor while Nick looked around to see if he was being watched. As Artemis and Curie readied the hole, Nick prepared the decoy. He pulled the old circuit board from his pocket and placed it in a plastic bag, just like the one Artemis used for the real device.

Curie stopped digging and Artemis dropped to one knee. He pushed a button on the Masters' Motion Sensor, and then carefully placed it in the hole. After piling dirt on top, he stuck a small plastic orange flag in the mound.

While Artemis was satisfied, Nick was not. He waited patiently for his dad and Curie to head back to the van. When the coast was clear, he quickly dug a shallow hole, then buried the fake device. Nick took a mental picture of where the Masters' Motion Sensor was, and moved the flag to the fake one. He dusted himself off, and then ran back the van.

"Why did you do that?" asked Curie.

"You saw that, huh?" Nick said, then handed the wrapper to his sister. "Look at this."

She did. The chocolate was still gooey. "It doesn't make sense. Why would this new candy bar wrapper be inside this closed off area?" wondered Curie.

"See that black car over there? I think they've been following us since we left San Francisco," Nick said.

Curie slowly turned around, and pretended to tie her shoelace. She snuck a peek, but a newspaper hid the faces in the car. "Who do you think it is?" she asked.

"I don't know, but since they're hiding their faces, I don't think they're friends of ours," said Nick. He put the laptop back in the van.

"Don't put that away just yet," said Curie.

"Why?" asked Nick, as he pulled the laptop back.

"I'll show you," said Curie. She took the laptop from Nick and turned it on.

Artemis was just about ready to start the van when he looked over and saw that the co-pilot chair was empty. "Pilot to co-pilot...uhm, where are you?" asked Artemis. He saw both Nick and Curie in the backseat, laptop between them. "Isn't it your turn to sit up here, Curie?" asked Artemis.

"Yes, Dad, but Nick and I are working on something," said Curie.

"But who's going to kick the tires and light the fires?" asked Artemis. His voice wavered a bit, letting his kids know how much he missed their interaction.

"Can I do it from back here, Dad?" asked Curie.

"Sure, Curie," said Artemis. He flipped his sunglasses down. "Pilot to co-pilot. All systems go?"

"Roger that, captain," said Curie. "All systems are A-OK. Kick the tires and light the fires."

Artemis smiled, started the van, and put it into gear.

"Okay, so what did you want to show me?" asked Nick.

Curie pulled up the same website Nick had used to locate the old apartment building. "I was thinking that if we could find satellite photos from 1994, why couldn't we find them from today," she said.

"Curie, that is a great idea!" shouted Nick. "But what if they have some sort of secret password or something?"

"They do, it's a 'Member's Only' page, and thanks to Dad, we are members," said Curie. Her fingers flashed across the keyboard. "I'm going to track things back to our street address and check to see what, or who, was around us at the time we left," she added, as a satellite photograph of their street popped up on the computer screen.

"Get in closer," said Nick, eager to find out who was following them. Curie clicked a few keys and zoomed into their neighborhood. "There's our van!" said Nick, excited.

"And there's the black sedan," said Curie. She clicked the mouse button again, and brought the black sedan into full view. But instead of being able to see the people inside, all they saw was a copy of *Scientific Times* newspaper concealing their identity.

"Rats," said Curie.

"Maybe we can track them while we are driving," said Nick. "They can't hide behind a newspaper and drive at the same time."

"Great idea, Copernicus!" said Curie. She surfed through data, and clicked through frames until she came to a clear shot of the black sedan following their van. "I think we've got them!" She zeroed in on the car, getting closer and closer until she was right on the windshield. And clear as day was a picture of two people hidden behind dark sunglasses and big black hats. "Double rats!" said Curie, angry that they were let down by technology. "They could be anybody!"

"Maybe they're not even following us," said Nick. "Maybe some kid dropped a candy wrapper, and the wind blew it over the fence."

"Or maybe not," said Curie as she focused in on the dashboard of the black car. In plain view was the same kind of candy bar as the candy wrapper Nick found in the dirt lot.

Both Nick and Curie turned and looked out the back window, trying to find the black sedan they knew was out there.

CHAPTER FOUR:

BLANKET COVERAGE

The sun set over the Hollywood Hills, and the huge white letters spelling out "Hollywood" that towered over the city. Inside their motel room, Curie and Nick, already in their pajamas, moved suitcases, chairs and whatever they could find in front of the motel room door.

Artemis came out of the bathroom, sneezing terribly. "Someone had a dog in this room," he said, not seeing the obstacle in front of him. Before he could stop, Artemis had flipped head over heels and landed in a crumpled ball.

"Are you okay, Dad?" asked Curie.

He looked at his two children who stared down at him. "I'm not sure. Did I just trip over a pile of suitcases and chairs blocking the only way out of our motel room?" asked Artemis.

"Uhm, yeah," both kids said.

"Then I'm okay," said Artemis. He got to his feet, and then began to pull the mountain apart, still sneezing now and then. "You know, other than being a fire hazard, and not to mention tripping hazard, my allergy medicine is in the suitcase on the bottom," he said.

"Sorry, Dad. We were just playing a game," said Curie as she helped her dad unblock the door.

"But Curie, there are some bad men out there, and–" said Nick. Curie put her hand over her brother's mouth and forced a laugh.

"Ha ha, Nick. Game's over. Come on, and help us clean up," said Curie. Nick shot his sister a look, but quickly realized she was right. The trio cleared the doorway, and Artemis grabbed his suitcase and went back to the bathroom. When the coast was clear, both Curie and Nick peeked out the window. The black car was nowhere to be seen.

"Where do you think they are?" asked Nick.

"Hopefully on their way to Palm Springs," said Curie.

"Why Palm Springs?" asked Nick.

"Because it's far away from here," said Curie. Nick saw that she was scared.

"Don't worry, Curie. I won't let anything happen to you. I'll stay up all night in this chair and keep watch," said Nick. Curie smiled, happy to have such a brave brother.

"You'd do that for me?" asked Curie.

"Yeah, I guess so. I know you're older and everything, but I am a man. Well, almost, anyway," said Nick.

"Thanks, Copernicus," said Curie. Relieved, she crawled under the covers and pulled them up to her chin. But she didn't want to close her eyes. "Aren't you scared, too?" she asked.

"A little, I guess," said Nick, whose knees were pulled up to his chin. Every little sound caused him to jump. From the cars that drove by to the families unloading their luggage, his head darted this way and that. And when a motel room door slammed, he'd had enough. Like a jack-in-the-box, he popped up from the chair, flew across the room and tunneled under the covers next to his sister. Nick and Curie **cleaved** to each other, the blankets up so high they almost covered their eyes.

"Maybe we both should stay here in the bed, you know, to protect each other?" said Curie.

"I think that's a good idea," said Nick.

The kids tried really hard to stay awake, but were so tired from their trip that sleep quickly took over. Artemis came out of the bathroom, whistling a happy tune, unaware that his kids were asleep. When he saw them snuggled up in bed, he stopped his whistling and tiptoed over to them. Artemis stroked their hair and kissed them on the cheek. He went over to the window to make sure the alarm lights on the van were blinking. What he didn't see, though, were several dark sedans parked behind the van in the parking lot.

CHAPTER FIVE:

TREMORS

Nick woke up and stretched. Curie slept next to him almost the same way that she had the night before. He was just about to tickle her awake, when he noticed their dad was not in his bed. And it didn't look like he even slept in it!

"Curie!" cried Nick.

Curie bolted up. "What, what?" she said, still foggy with sleep. "Is there an earthquake?" She rolled out of bed and stumbled toward the bathroom doorway for protection.

"No, Curie. Dad's missing!" he squeaked.

Curie rubbed her eyes and looked at Artemis' bed. It was perfectly made as if no one had slept in it at all. A little bit nervous, she looked in the bathroom. Nope, Artemis was not there either, and neither were his bags!

"Curie, do you think those guys—" Curie cut Nick off.

"No way! Couldn't be. There has to be a logical explanation," said Curie. But she wasn't so sure.

"Like space aliens zapping him away?" asked Nick. "I knew we should've barricaded the door," he added, not wanting to cry.

Curie, the older of the two, knew it was her job to remain calm. Sure, Nick was tall for his age, but he was still just a kid. With their dad not there, Curie had to be the one in charge.

"Nick, you're a scientist. Act like one!" lectured Curie. But she could see in his eyes that right now he was a boy who missed his dad. Her resolve wavered. Maybe he was right. It was time to act like a kid.

"You should've stayed awake. You should've watched that door!" barked Curie.

"You could have helped me!" Nick shot back.

They both screamed as the door opened. Artemis nearly jumped out of his skin as his children stared at him, wide-eyed.

"What? Is it my shirt? I knew it didn't match, but it's my favorite. Maybe I should change it?" said Artemis.

"Dad, where were you? We thought the worst!" said Curie.

"I was loading up the van. We've got a big day ahead of us. An 8.5 magnitude day in fact," said Artemis, as he looked at his shirt in the mirror.

"But your bed wasn't slept in, and...wait a minute. What do you mean an 8.5 magnitude day? Is there an earthquake coming?" asked Nick.

"It's good luck to make your bed the first day of a trip," Artemis said, and smiled coyly. "And yes, there is an earthquake coming. If we don't get going, we're going to miss it," he added.

"Missing it is a good thing, isn't it?" said Curie, not sure what to think.

"That depends. The best way to understand something you're studying is to experience it. Either in its natural state, or in controlled conditions," said Artemis, adjusting the glasses perched on his nose.

"Dad, you can't really make an earthquake, can you?" asked Nick. He wondered if his dad was more of a genius than he knew.

"No, I can't, but Universal Studios can," said Artemis.

Suddenly, the kids got it. "We're going to Universal Studios Theme Park!" they shouted. Nick and Curie forgot all about their fears, and quickly got dressed.

They both ran as fast as they could, focused on one desire—being the first one to the van so they could sit in Command-Com. They were neck and neck as Nick's long legs helped him match Curie's speed. Their hands grasped the door handle at the same time. Nick tried to open the door just as his dad clicked on the remote to unlock the doors. Every door opened but that one.

Curie, seeing the opening to win the seat, darted to the side door. Nick quickly followed and bounded into the van right after Curie. They were so focused on getting into the seat they didn't realize that something had stuck to each of their shoes.

"I'll get here first next time," said Nick.

"Not as long as you're racing against me," said Curie as she buckled her seat belt.

Nick sat down in the back seat, not seeing the candy bar wrapper and piece of paper that had fallen off the soles of their shoes.

CHAPTER SIX:

A WHOLE LOTTA SHAKING GOING ON

   Universal Studios Theme Park drew Nick in like a strong magnet. He beamed with excitement as they stepped through the gates. Everywhere he looked there was something magical. Pirates on their way to some sort of fabulous movie adventure were followed by astronauts, the Three Little Pigs, and a huge boulder being carried by a petite woman. Nick turned in a circle, trying to take in all the fantasy worlds that collided around him.

   "Millions, maybe billions of movies were made here!" said Nick.

   "More like thousands," said Curie, not caught up in the moment like her brother. She wanted to get

down to business. "Dad, where is the earthquake ride?"

But Artemis didn't answer. He too was fascinated by the unbelievable world of Hollywood. Curie grabbed Artemis and Nick by the hand and led them toward the sign that read: *Universal Studios Hollywood Studio Tour.*

Loaded onto the tram, which was similar to an open-air bus with the cars connected together, Artemis, Curie and Nick settled in for the adventure. While they were there only to experience an earthshaking, groundbreaking, breathtaking earthquake, the back lot tour took them through a whole different world of movie making wonder. A giant shark nipped at their heels, a city was devastated beyond imagination by a war of the worlds, and a great ape named King Kong towered above them.

"Are we almost there, Dad?" asked Curie, who would much rather be in the thick of things.

Artemis didn't hear Curie. His mind was elsewhere. He was **euphoric** from everything going on around him. Everywhere they turned something amazing was happening. "Did you see the size of that shark?" said Artemis.

"How about that monkey? He was huger than huge," said Nick.

"The shark was fake, and the monkey is a gorilla, and he's fake too," said Curie.

Artemis sensed Curie was not enjoying the tour as much as he and Nick were. "I know you want to go through the earthquake, and we'll get there soon enough," said Artemis.

"But we're here for work, not for fun, Dad," said Curie.

"In our business, Curie, work is fun. How many people get to study the wild and crazy things of the world?" he asked.

"Ooh, I know, I know!" said Nick, throwing up his hand.

"That was a rhetorical question, Copernicus," said Curie.

"But I still know the answer. It's us!" Nick said as he high-fived his dad.

Curie had to smile at her brother and father who were having the time of their lives. "That shark was pretty scary, wasn't it?" said Curie.

"It sure was!" said Nick, who pretended to be a shark and nipped at her shoulder.

Just then, the ride announcer told them to prepare for the unexpected as they relived an 8.5 magnitude earthquake.

"Well, it's going to get much scarier very soon!" said Artemis. He was very excited, and maybe just a little bit nervous. Nick and Curie moved closer to their father, who put his arms around them and hugged them tightly.

The doors opened, and the tram crept into a make-believe subway tunnel, into the world of the unknown. Suddenly, everything went black, and a deep voice called out, "It's just a tremor. There is no danger."

But the voice was wrong! The ground shook uncontrollably. The tram lurched from side to side, making everyone feel like an egg ready to be cracked into a frying pan.

Though they knew it was just a ride, Nick and Curie squeezed as close to Artemis as they could get. And just in time. Steel and concrete groaned as the ground rose and fell uncontrollably, just like the earth's crust in a real earthquake. They quickly turned to see sparks from broken electrical cable light up the subway tunnel like a fireworks show. Then fire

erupted from broken gas lines. The heat warmed their faces as the flames shot upward.

The howl of the tunnel as it stretched and pulled was so loud it felt like it was in their bones! Screams pierced the darkness, as everyone felt helpless. Without warning, the ceiling caved in and a giant gasoline truck slid toward the tram from the gaping hole that opened in a street above them.

Curie and Nick grabbed their father and held him tightly. They were on a collision course with disaster! Curie covered her eyes. Nick kept one eye open as the truck stopped just short of hitting the tram. It burst into flames, causing the whole room to light up. Even Artemis let out a scream.

The sights and sounds came from everywhere. Sirens cried in the distance as emergency vehicles responded. Just when Curie wondered how it could get any worse, a water main broke, sending thousands of gallons of water whooshing towards them. By now, everyone had forgotten it was just a ride, and screamed as if they were living through a real earthquake!

Finally, the chaos slowed. The shaking stopped and the lights gradually came up. A voice proclaimed, "Congratulations, you have successfully survived an 8.5 magnitude earthquake!" Wide-eyed, the exhausted kids focused straight ahead as the tram pulled out of the ride. The only thing they wanted to do now was get back on solid ground.

Sitting outside on a lovely summer day, Nick, Curie and Artemis licked their ice cream cones as the sticky mix ran down the sides. Ice cream helped. There is something about the cool, sweet concoction that soothes the soul even on the toughest of days. Living through an 8.5 magnitude earthquake, even if it's fake, needs some comforting.

"I didn't think it would be like that," Curie said, still shaken by the experience.

"I didn't know what to expect," Nick added.

"Well, Hollywood made it a little more dramatic, but a lot of those things do happen," said Artemis. "Just not always in the same place at the same time."

"I felt so helpless," said Nick.

"Me, too," agreed Curie.

Artemis flipped up his sunglasses, put down his ice cream cone, and gave his kids his full attention.

"It is scary, I know, but there are things we can do to be better prepared for an earthquake," he said.

"You already told us about retrofitting buildings, and standing in the doorway and stuff like that," said Curie.

"That's all well and good, but there are things we can do for ourselves," said Artemis.

"Like what?" asked Nick.

"For one, having an Earthquake Survival Kit makes a big difference," said Artemis.

"That sounds like a first aid kit," said Nick.

"It is, sort of. It contains a lot of things you need after an earthquake happens," said Artemis. "A gallon of water a day for each person, a first aid kit, canned food."

The kids forgot about their fear, and got excited about what they could do to be better prepared for an earthquake.

"You'd need a can opener," said Nick.

"How about a portable radio or TV? Those are good things to have, too, right?" asked Curie.

"And flashlights, blankets to keep warm and extra eyeglasses if you need them. The goal is to be prepared," said their dad.

"Is that why you taught Nick and me how to turn off the gas, water and electricity?" asked Curie.

"And why you made us memorize all those emergency numbers?" asked Nick.

"Yes, and why all the really heavy things we own are down low, and why the bookcases are bolted to the walls," said Artemis.

"An earthquake doesn't seem as scary when you're prepared for it," said Nick.

"I am glad you understand," said Artemis.

"So, where are we off to now?" asked Curie.

"I was thinking we should probably just go home, you know, we've had as much fun as anybody can have," said Artemis.

"What? Are you kidding?" asked Nick.

"The adventure has just begun," said Curie.

Artemis pretended to be deep in thought. "Well, there are a lot of pressing things that need to be taken care of at home. Someone has to take out the garbage, and I think there's a gallon of milk that is about to expire," he said. He watched the sad faces of his kids, and then changed gears. "The heck with it. The garbage will take care of itself, and the milk will become cottage cheese!"

Both kids shouted with joy, and then jumped on their dad, giving him a great big bear hug.

"I didn't know you kids loved cottage cheese so much," said Artemis.

Curie looked up at her dad. "No, Dad, we love you that much."

"And more," said Nick, squeezing Artemis tighter.

"Well, we've got a big adventure ahead of us, so we'd better get on the road," said Artemis. He tried to stand, but the kids had him in a never-ending hug.

CHAPTER SEVEN:

WIPE YOUR FEET BEFORE YOU TAKE YOUR SEAT

Curie and Nick looked like track stars as they raced towards the Masters of Disasters van. Who would be first to the van? Neck and neck they ran, separated by only a breath. This time, Nick had a slight lead, and got there first.

"I told you I'd win," said Nick, out of breath.

"I let you beat me," said Curie, who was only a second behind her brother.

They both climbed into the van. As Curie buckled up, something on the floor caught her eye. It was a candy bar wrapper and a smudged piece of paper. She took a deep breath, then picked them up. What she saw surprised her.

"Nick. Hey, Nick." Curie whispered. There was no response from Nick, who was flipping through CDs. "Copernicus!" Curie's raised voice got Nick's attention.

"What?" he asked.

"Come here, please," Curie said.

"No way. I won fair and square," he said.

Curie looked over to see her dad getting into the van, then quickly flashed Nick the candy bar wrapper and piece of paper. Nick realized Curie was serious. She had another clue to the puzzle. Nick unbuckled his seat belt, and moved to the back seat.

"How did those get in here?" asked Nick. He took the candy bar wrapper and the paper. His eyes opened wide when he saw what was written on the paper. A series of hieroglyphic-looking numbers and mathematical formulas stared back at him. If you didn't have a scientific mind, you'd think they were the writings of a madman, but Nick and Curie knew better.

"Is that the Masters' Motion Sensor formula?" Curie asked, a little nervous about the answer.

"It's only part of it. They got a lot of it wrong," Nick replied. He turned to his dad, who was just buckling his seat belt. "Hey, uh, Dad, have you been experimenting with a new formula for the Masters' Motion Sensor?" he asked cautiously.

"No. Research is right on the nose," Artemis said as he started up the van.

"Maybe it's an old version of the formula that somehow got left in the van," Curie said, hoping to explain away the mystery.

Nick flipped over the torn piece of paper. He saw his shoe print, plus part of the name of a school: POLY-TECH.

"No, this is from a Tech University. Dad went to Harvard," said Nick.

Curie rubbed the candy wrapper between her fingers. "The chocolate is dry. We could have picked them up anywhere," said Curie.

Nick peeked out the window. "Who are these guys?"

"And what do they want?" Curie added.

CHAPTER EIGHT:

GETTING THERE IS HALF THE FUN, SORT OF...

The Masters of Disasters van was stuck in rush hour traffic along with hundreds of other cars. In the distance a sign read: *Nevada State Line, 386 miles.*

Inside the van, Nick and Curie sat on the couch, eyes glued to the laptop.

"Did you get the satellite signal yet?" Nick asked.

"No, it's still down," Curie replied. She reached into her backpack and pulled out a notebook. "Okay, we have plenty of time. Let's figure out who is following us and why," she said.

"It's the CIA," said Nick.

"The Central Intelligence Agency?" asked Curie.

"Of course, they found out how smart we are, and they want us to teach them everything we know," said Nick.

"I must be asleep, because I am having the funniest dream, and you're in it," said Curie.

"Yeah, what's it about?" asked Nick, playfully.

"You really are a boy, aren't you?" said Curie.

"It took you this long to figure that out? Maybe the CIA only wants to talk to me?" said Nick.

Curie took out a pen and opened her notebook. "Let's get serious, okay?" she said. "Now we know that someone has been following us since San Francisco. The question is why."

"It sure looks like they want to steal Dad's invention," said Nick.

"Dad's security system is top notch," added Curie.

They both looked down at the cryptic notes on the paper. The formula was too close to their dad's. "But how do we explain this?" Nick wondered out loud.

"Every security has its weakness, which is probably why they're trying to get to it while we're on the road," said Curie.

"Do they want the laptops, or do they want the Masters' Motion Sensor devices?" wondered Nick. "One doesn't work without the other. I mean, you can transmit information, but without the program to interpret the data, it's useless," he added.

"You're right," Curie said. "It makes perfect sense. Do we tell Dad?"

Before Nick could respond, Artemis jerked his head like a dog that saw a cat run across the lawn.

"Did you feel that?" asked Artemis. "I think it was a 1.8 on the Richter scale," he added.

"You mean we just had an earthquake?" asked Nick.

"Or maybe an aftershock. It is possible we missed the earthquake," said Artemis. "Though I doubt it. I am in tune with them."

Both kids scrambled to the front of the van as Artemis turned on the high frequency scanner. He scanned through the stations until he came to a news announcer who told about the earthquake that just hit.

"Just outside of Los Angeles, residents felt a little jolt today as a 1.8 magnitude earthquake just rolled through," said the radio announcer.

"Wow, Dad, you were right on," said Nick proudly.

"Well, disasters are my business," Artemis said as he smiled.

"Dad, that can only mean that you're right on track with your assumption that a big quake is coming," said Curie.

"Maybe sooner than later," said Nick.

"You kids might be right, but nature is unpredictable. We've got to use our scientific minds, and expand our tracking of fault lines until we figure out just when and where the next big earthquake is going to hit!" said Artemis.

Nick and Curie looked at each other.

"And make sure that the Masters' Motion Sensors stay safe," said Curie to her brother.

CHAPTER NINE:

HERE, THERE...
UH, NOWHERE!

The sleepy little town of Pleasant Valley, Nevada looked nothing like its name. The rocky terrain, jutting mountains and cactus made it look inviting only to snakes, scorpions, and coyotes. The Masters of Disaster van pulled up to the lone filling station where a rusty sign swung in the wind. Artemis looked in the back and saw that the children were asleep. He stepped out to stretch and look around.

Coming from San Francisco, where almost every square inch is covered with concrete, asphalt or a building, the Masters family was truly in the middle of nowhere. Clem, an old timer who looked like he could be a cowboy from the Old West, lounged in a chair in front of the filling station office.

"We're outta gas," said Clem.

"That's okay, we don't need any," said Artemis. "But my cell phone isn't working out here. Do you have a phone I could use?"

"Sure thing. Right through them doors," said Clem.

Artemis looked back in the van to see the kids still sleeping, and went to the office.

Curie was the first to wake up. Not seeing her dad, she shook Nick.

Still half asleep, he flailed his arms around. "What? No. Stop. You can't have it," said Nick. He looked up to see it was just Curie.

"Dad's gone," she said.

Nick was now fully awake. He and Curie bounded out of the van, and landed right in front of Clem.

"Who are you?" asked Curie.

"I'm Clem," he said politely.

"Where's our dad?" Nick asked.

"Well, if he's a tall gentleman with about five pairs of glasses, he just went to use the phone," Clem replied.

Nick looked around, making sure they were safe. "Have you seen any black cars come through here today?" he asked.

"We don't get too many cars through these parts," said Clem. "Been here 97 years, and I could probably count every car I've seen."

"Wow, you're old," said Nick.

"Thank you very much, son," said Clem.

Curie pulled her notebook out of her backpack. "Then you were probably here for the earthquake of 1915," she said.

"Yes I was, and I remember it like it was yesterday," said Clem. "If you think there's nothing here now, you should've seen it then. Tumbleweeds and a few adobe homes, but that's a good thing. You see, that earthquake shook at what them scientists said was a 7.1 magnitude."

"Were you scared?" asked Curie.

"You bet I was," Clem replied.

"Was anybody hurt?" asked Nick.

"Thank the good Lord, no. Like I said, weren't many folks living here back then," said Clem.

"Why didn't you just leave?" asked Nick.

Clem rubbed his chin and laughed. "It's not like it is now with cars and planes that will take you anywhere you want to go. No, we stayed because we had to stay, and we made the best of it," he added.

"I'm sure you did," said Artemis, as he walked out the filling station door. "That earthquake also changed the flow of springs and streams throughout northern Nevada," he added.

"If it never happened, people might be coming by for more than a bathroom break," said Clem. "Things are pretty dry in these parts."

"Well, we better be getting on our way. Thanks for your help," said Artemis.

"You folks take care," said Clem.

Artemis climbed back into the van, but Nick and Curie took their time. They scanned the desert for the black sedan.

"Looks like they're on their way to Palm Springs," said Curie. She climbed into the van, but Nick wasn't so sure.

The van carefully followed a seldom-used trail. The dips and bumps almost made it feel like a slow-moving roller coaster. Artemis parked the van,

and unloaded the equipment with the kids' help. They all moved quickly, having done this twice already.

Even though there was no one around for miles, Nick buried a fake monitoring device and moved the flag just like before.

"You still think we're being followed?" asked Curie.

"I just want to be safe," said Nick.

Back at the filling station, Clem sat in his chair as a cloud of dust moved toward him. When it was almost upon the filling station, he stood and walked to the pumps.

"We're out of gas," he said as the black sedan came to a stop.

CHAPTER TEN:

ROLLING THROUGH NO MAN'S LAND

The desert wind whipped through the dry sand and made the scorching heat a little more bearable. The Masters of Disasters van raced along the two-lane highway through the tiny town of Kosmo, Utah and toward Hansel Valley, a lightly populated area that was the site of Utah's largest earthquake.

Curie sat in the front seat and read the pages on her laptop. "This earthquake occurred in 1934, in the lightly populated area of Hansel Valley," she said. "While property damage was minor, two people were killed." Curie stopped reading, touched by the loss of life. "Wow, you sort of forget that real things happen to real people when you're focused on the research," she said.

"Do you see now why the work we do is so important?" asked Artemis.

"Yes, all the things we learn help everyone handle a natural disaster," said Nick.

"What are we going to learn about here, Dad?" asked Curie.

"This is a really interesting site. One that I think will really help in collecting data with the Masters' Motion Sensors," said Artemis.

The van came to a stop not far from a hill. Artemis, Curie and Nick all jumped out, and then quickly scrambled for their equipment.

"Please bring the camera this time, Curie," said Artemis. Curie grabbed the camera as Nick grabbed more equipment than he could handle. He struggled to carry the load, then spun in a circle and fell to the ground.

"Let me help you," said Curie.

"I can do it," said Nick. But he really couldn't. He struggled and fought while Curie watched and waited.

"Okay, I can use your help!" said Nick.

"All you had to do was ask," said Curie, as she picked up some of the pieces.

The two kids struggled up to where Artemis had already begun to study the land. He looked through a square made by holding up his fingers together. The kids stopped and put the equipment down carefully. What greeted them was amazing. Channels cut in the earth still showed the outlines of the scarps, which are lines of cliffs formed by the faulting or fracturing of the earth's crust after an earthquake. While not huge, they were a reminder of just how powerful an earthquake can be, even in the middle of nowhere.

"Do you want me to take a picture of those scarps, Dad?" asked Curie.

"No, thanks," said Artemis. "I want to take a picture of both you and Nick standing next to them." The two carefully stepped over to the scarps, as if the ground could open up at any moment. Below them, ants danced across a candy wrapper. Nick didn't see it, but Curie did. Shocked, she bent down and picked it up as Nick talked to their father.

"What magnitude was the earthquake that made this, Dad?" asked Nick.

"It was a 6.6," said Artemis.

Curie showed Nick the candy wrapper.

"No way," said Nick.

"Yeah, I know," said Artemis as he snapped a few pictures. "Earthquakes are everywhere. Isn't that cool?"

"Hey, Dad, can I use the camera?" Curie asked.

"Make sure you get my good side," Artemis joked as he handed her the camera.

"Now, what I want to do here is place three Masters' Motion Sensors about twenty feet apart along this scarp," said Artemis, who started marking his locations.

But the kids weren't listening to him. Their concern was how the candy wrapper got there.

"Look," Curie said, "this is the first place we've been able to see clear footprints." She pointed to the ground where footprints crisscrossed each other, then snapped some pictures.

"Do you think Clem lied to us? I mean, maybe he's in on it, too," said Nick, worried.

"I don't think so. Logically, it doesn't make sense," said Curie. "He has no reason to lie, nothing to gain, and if he really wanted to steal the Masters'

Motion Sensing Device he would have done it while Dad was away from the van," she added.

"You're right. They must have come at night. But why?" asked Nick.

Curie looked over to her father huddled near the ground. "How many decoys do you have left, Nick?" asked Curie.

"I don't know," said Nick. He looked out on the horizon to see if there were any cars coming.

"Come on, Nick. This is no time to be afraid," said Curie. "Where is the brother who was going to protect me from the bad guys?" she asked.

"He hid under the sheets, remember?" Nick replied.

"And I was right there with you," said Curie. "We can do this together."

Nick went through his backpack. "I only have two left," he said.

"No, you have three," Curie said as she took off her "Best Friends for Life" friendship bracelet given to her by her best friend, Bella.

"Curie, I can't take that," said Nick.

"This is more important," said Curie. "I might have more best friends, but I only have one brother and dad."

"Thanks, Curie," said Nick as he gladly took the bracelet, happy to have such a cool sister.

As Artemis sat under a shade tree with his laptop, Curie and Nick quickly dug holes in the sand, and put the orange marker flags over the decoys.

"What are we going to tell Dad?" asked Curie.

"That depends on if the Masters' Motion Sensor program is working or not," said Nick.

"What do you mean?" asked Curie.

"If it's not working, then the bad guys have dug up the real devices, and not the fake ones," Nick said.

They walked up behind their father to see the words: WARNING: MOVEMENT ALONG THE FAULT LINE! flash across the computer screen.

Artemis was like a little kid at Christmas, staring at the screen as if Santa Claus brought him the Red Ryder BB gun he had been asking for all year. "It's working...it is working..." he said under his breath. He looked up and saw his children. "Kids, this is bigger than I thought. It's picking up movement not only on the San Andreas Fault, but on the New Madrid Fault line as well," he spouted happily.

"But Dad, the New Madrid fault is in Missouri," Curie said.

"I know! Isn't that cool?" Artemis said as he stood up. "In 1812, one of the strongest earthquakes ever felt struck New Madrid, Missouri," he explained. His hands swung around, animating his words. "Large holes in the ground called fissures opened and swallowed massive quantities of river and marsh water. And when they closed again, huge amounts of mud and sand were shot into the air, covering everything around them! Boy, what I would give to have been there," Artemis added.

"Dad, you would have been killed," Curie said with compassion. "The only reason there wasn't more loss of life back then is because hardly anyone lived there," she added.

Artemis looked at his kids. He knew they were right, but the love of his job made his passion seem crazy at times. "I was speaking figuratively, meaning to see such a thing would be a wonder for a scientist," he explained. He grabbed both his kids in a bear hug.

Nick and Curie looked at each other. The invention sure seemed to be working. But something nagged at them. They had evidence that something just wasn't right. The candy bar wrappers, the weird scientific note and the men following them in the car that now seemed to be ahead of them. What did it all mean?

CHAPTER ELEVEN:

THERE SHE BLOWS!

Artemis smiled as he watched the water shoot high into the sky from Old Faithful, like a whale blowing seawater out of its blowhole. Nick and Curie, though, were more interested in earthquakes and mystery men trying to steal their dad's invention.

"What are we doing here?" Curie wanted to know.

They both looked over at Artemis who acted more childlike than his kids.

"Did you know that Old Faithful used to erupt every 61 minutes before a 7.1 magnitude earthquake hit Montana in 1959?" asked Artemis gleefully. "All the geysers were either created or changed because of that earthquake," he added.

"That's great, Dad," Curie said, then turned to her brother. "The only way we're going to solve this mystery is on our own."

"But we can't leave Dad here, Curie. And anyway, someone needs to drive," Nick said.

Curie rolled her eyes. As smart as her brother was, sometimes the child in him took over. She pointed to a brochure about the park's Junior Ranger program. Nick got it.

"Hey Dad, Nick and I were thinking that we want to become Junior Rangers," she said.

Artemis looked at the brochure that detailed all the adventures kids could have while learning about Yellowstone National Park.

"I think that's a great idea," Artemis said. "In order to totally understand why there are earthquakes, you need to understand the earth. Come on, let's go!" he said.

Curie looked up at her dad. He was as eager as could be, and she felt bad telling him he couldn't come. "Well, we were going to do it on our own," she said.

"You're right. It's Junior Rangers, not Senior Rangers," Artemis said as he laughed at his own joke.

"You kids go have fun, and I'm going back to the van to work on the Masters' Motion Sensors program." Artemis ruffled their hair and walked to the van.

Nick looked at the brochure, and then at his sister. "We don't have time to do this," said Nick.

"But it gives us the time alone to figure out just what is going on here," Curie said.

Nick leafed through the Junior Rangers brochure. "I'd really like to get one of those patches, though," he said. "Hey, look. You can learn about bears!"

Curie grabbed her brother by the arm. "Come on, Copernicus."

But before they could set out on their own adventure, they were swallowed up by a crush of children all wanting to become Junior Rangers.

Nick and Curie fidgeted as they stood in front of a park ranger with a large ranger's hat, socks folded over his boots, and shorts that bulged at the knees.

Curie leaned over and whispered in her brother's ear. "Let's go."

A loud shriek from a ranger's whistle turned their attention back to the park ranger.

"Attention, young men and women!" said the park ranger. "In 1872, President Ulysses S. Grant signed the act that made Yellowstone the first national park in the United States of America, thereby protecting it for the benefit and enjoyment of the people. You, being the people, are here to become Junior Rangers. To do that, you will need to pass certain tests to receive this patch. When sewn onto the shirt of your choice, it will show the world that you, Mr. Boy or Ms. Girl, have met all the requirements to do so! Is that understood?" barked the park ranger.

"Yes, Sir!" All the children shouted as they stared at the colored patch with Junior Ranger, Yellowstone embroidered on it.

The other kids laughed and scattered around like a pen full of crazy chickens, but Curie and Nick stayed put. They were now on their own quest.

"Where should we start?" asked Nick.

"Right here," said Curie, as she pointed to the snack bar on their map. "If the candy bar theory holds up, they've been there," she added.

The two headed off to the snack bar where a tall, lanky teenager worked behind the counter. He stared at the old candy wrappers sealed tight in a Ziploc bag. Curie grilled him like she was a trial attorney and he was their main witness.

"Have you sold any of this brand of candy bar today?" Curie barked.

The lanky teenager's eyes darted between the candy wrappers and Curie. "Yeah, sure, it's only like the best selling candy bar in the world," he quipped sarcastically.

Nick held up a sketch, much like a police drawing, of two men in dark glasses and hats. "Did anyone matching this description buy any of those candy bars?" he asked.

The lanky teenager squinted, studied the picture, and then looked like he recognized the picture. "Yeah, there were six people who looked like the guys in that picture," he said.

Nick and Curie looked at each other.

"Six? Are you sure it's not two?" Nick asked.

"Little guy, part of my job is numbers," the teen replied. "I'm like zoned in on the digits. I sell the stuff and make the change. Dollars, quarters, nickels, dimes and pennies. I know the difference between two and six," he added.

Curie and Nick exchanged a worried look. This isn't what they expected. Six is not the same as two, and if their witness was right, their theory wasn't.

"Thank you very much," Curie said and she turned and walked toward a picnic table. Nick followed and sat down next to her.

"If there are six, then that would explain how they can be all around us," said Nick.

"But why would there be six of them? It doesn't make any sense," thought Curie.

"Nothing makes sense," said Nick. "Every time the Masters' Motion Sensor program is run on the computer it warns us about movement on the fault line."

"Either Dad's invention doesn't work, or these guys are really good," added Curie.

"Let's figure out which," said Nick.

They laid out their evidence. The candy wrappers, note, picture of the footprints and the pencil drawing of the two men.

"They've been following us since San Francisco, but haven't tried to take the Masters' Motion Sensors," said Curie.

"Their best chance would have been in Pleasant Valley, Nevada," added Nick.

"There must be something more important to them than taking Dad's invention," said Curie.

"It has to be the research," said Curie. "But the one thing I can't figure out is how they seem to know where we're going even before we get there," she added.

"The GPS!" shouted Nick. "Every time it connects with the Global Positioning Satellite, it tells them exactly where we are," he added.

"And they're able to use their computers to see where we're going," said Curie.

Nick kicked the ground, thinking, when he noticed footprints right in front of him. He looked at the photograph of the footprints. Nick showed Curie they matched perfectly.

"Let's track these guys," said Nick.

Curie looked at him like he was crazy. "We don't know anything about them," she said.

"This is the best way to find out. Come on, we can really be Junior Rangers then," Nick said.

"You just want that patch," Curie said.

Nick smiled. That might have been the case, but his need for the truth surpassed his desire for that patch.

The kids walked around the park like the dozens of other children following animal tracks. But Nick and Curie were tracking potential bad guys who wanted to do bad things. Their journey seemed to take them in circles. What they quickly learned was that the lanky teenager at the concession stand was right. There were six different men who fit the description. Though they all wore the same style of shoe, there were six different sizes.

"It looks like they're walking a beat." said Curie.

"What do you mean, Curie?" her brother said.

"Like what policemen do when they're trying to protect an area," she said.

"Protect an area?" Nick mumbled to himself. He gazed around the park. His mind flashed back to the different places they'd been. Curie seemed to be doing the same thing, as she studied the bag of candy bar wrappers.

"Nick, you don't think that they're here to protect us, and not to try and steal Dad's invention, do you?" Curie asked.

Nick did. His shoulders slumped. "We've been chasing the wrong clues!" he shouted.

"No, we haven't. It just means we're safe," his sister said. "They're just really messy people, and Dad's invention works," Curie added.

"You forgot about this." Nick held up the paper that had Poly-Tech on one side, and a formula eerily similar to their dad's. "If someone is up to no good, I want to know who it is."

CHAPTER TWELVE:

PEDAL TO THE MEDDLE

Road signs flew by as the van drove through Wyoming and into Nebraska. The sun had set, and the line of cars following them all had their headlights on. Inside the van, Artemis sang along to a favorite old song on the radio. He got half the words right, but didn't care either way.

The kids sat in the back, looking out the rear window. There were lots of cars, but they couldn't tell if any of them were black. Curie was tired. Her eyes hung heavy, and she wanted to sleep.

"Don't you see? These guys were hired to protect us...well, protect Dad, and his invention," Nick said.

"Then why didn't Dad tell us?" asked Curie.

"Curie, sometimes he forgets that he put the car keys in the ignition," said Nick. "He's got so much going on in his mind, it's amazing he remembers his name," he added as he turned around, and leaned his head on the back of the seat.

"Then we should tell him about the formula we found," said Curie, "so he can decide what to do about it."

"No way, Curie," Nick answered. "What if he decides to stop this whole earthquake experiment all together? Then all his time and research will be for nothing," said Nick. He was tired, and his tone of voice made that perfectly clear.

"Well, if we're not going to tell Dad, then we really have to solve this problem on our own," said Curie. "But how?"

Nick's response was a snore. Curie looked over at her brother, who was fast asleep. She wanted to stay awake, and she fought hard, but the humming of the road became hypnotic. Soon, she too was snoring next to her brother.

CHAPTER THIRTEEN:

I SCREAM, YOU SCREAM, WE ALL SCREAM FOR THE HOME TEAM

"Wake up, sleepyheads. We're on the home stretch," Artemis shouted a little too cheerily. Sunshine spilled in on Curie and Nick as he pulled open the drapes.

They were still wearing the same clothes as the day before, and the Sandman had loaded an extra dose of sleep into their eyes.

Nick pulled his pillow over his head. "If we're so close to Missouri, why are we going home to stretch?" he said dreamily.

"Come on, you two. New Madrid, Missouri is calling our names," Artemis cried out, trying to arouse a little enthusiasm in his kids.

"Tell them we'll call back later," Curie said as she snuggled down deeper into the sheets.

Artemis crossed his arms and smiled at Nick and Curie. "Well, I tried to do this the nice way, but..." Artemis reached down and snatched the covers off the bed. Both Nick and Curie shot straight up.

"Dad!" they both shouted, none too happy.

"What?" Artemis asked with a playful smirk.

"That is so-o-o not cool," Curie said.

"What's not cool is that we still have two hours left to drive, and we haven't had breakfast yet," Artemis countered.

Curie crept to her feet, then moved in a **languid** manner toward the bathroom to brush her teeth. "Do we have to study any earthquakes here?" asked Curie.

"You sound like you're tired of it," said Artemis.

"Just tired, Dad," said Curie as she closed the bathroom door.

"How about you, Nick, tired of the adventure?" asked Artemis. Nick's reply was a short burst of snoring.

Artemis smiled, and then packed up his suitcase.

The trio dragged their suitcases toward the van. Out of the corner of their eyes, Nick and Curie spotted two black sedans sitting at the end of the parking lot. Their feet moved them forward, but their eyes drifted back, keeping watch on the cars.

"It's kind of cool having your own personal bodyguard, isn't it?" asked Curie.

"I feel like a rock star," added Nick.

The two clambered into the van. Artemis put it in gear and the family rumbled through Lincoln, Nebraska.

"They're still back there," said Nick, as he looked out the back window.

"And they'll be there the next time you look, too," Curie said, maybe just a little too curtly. But to her defense, she didn't get much sleep. Nick slid over next to his sister. She was still looking over their evidence.

"What are you worried about, Curie?" Nick asked. "It's over. Nothing's going to happen while all those guys are there." But Curie wasn't so sure, and this stirred Nick's interest.

"Why would there be only half a formula?" Curie asked. "And why would the Masters' Motion Sensor program always have the same alert?"

Nick was now into matching wits with his sister. "You're right. If there was that much movement across the fault line, the world would split in two," Nick said. "But how could Dad miss the obvious?"

Nick's question was quickly answered by his father. "Has anyone seen my sunglasses?" Artemis asked.

Curie and Nick looked and saw them sitting atop his head. "On your head, Dad," they both said. They fully understood how the absent-minded professor could overlook this. He was so focused on the end result, he didn't see what was right in front of him.

"What are we going to do?" asked Curie.

Nick's eyes went as wide as saucers. He had an idea!

"What? What?" Curie barked. She just had to know.

"Information is sent from the Masters' Motion Sensor, right?" asked Nick.

"Right," Curie agreed.

"Then why can't we track them?" asked Nick.

"Nick, you're brilliant!"   Curie said as she hugged her brother.

"I know," he said, only half joking.

Curie grabbed her laptop computer, slightly modified the Masters' Motion Sensor program in order to track the devices, then hit "enter." On the screen that showed a detailed map of the United States, blips of light marked where the devices were planted. They were all where they were supposed to be, except for one.

It seemed to be moving along the highway behind them!

CHAPTER FOURTEEN:

IF IT'S NOT ONE THING IT'S DEFINITELY THE OTHER

Artemis, Curie and Nick sat in a booth at Stauffer's Cafe and Pie Shoppe, a breakfast landmark in Lincoln, Nebraska. Nose stuck in his research, Artemis didn't notice his children's fascination with the parking lot. The kids were so distracted that when the breakfast order came they didn't even blink an eye.

Artemis dug right in, but soon noticed that his kids were there physically, but their minds were elsewhere. "Are you guys all right?" said Artemis.

"Yeah, sure, of course," both Nick and Curie said. They took a few bites of their meals, never taking their eyes off the parking lot.

Artemis took note of the odd behavior and tried to stir up the pot. "Wow, I did not know you could cook lizard this way," he observed.

The kids didn't seem to hear him, as they fumbled with their food, eyes locked to their work.

"It's a little crunchy. Must be the neck bone or maybe the feet," said Artemis. The kids still missed his comments, so he took it up a notch. "How is your eye of newt, Curie?" asked Artemis.

"Fine, thanks," said Curie, not really listening.

"And your frog nose is pretty good, Nick?" said Artemis.

"It's great, Dad, thanks," Nick said as he took a bite of his breakfast and almost missed his mouth.

Artemis was about to say something, when a blind man walked in with a seeing eye dog. The sneezing began slowly at first, and then became rapid fire. Artemis tried to tell Nick and Curie he was going out to the van to get his allergy medicine, but found that hand gestures worked better. He left the restaurant and went to the van.

Curie turned away from the window. Determined, she grabbed her father's laptop and spun it around so she could use it.

"What are you doing?" asked Nick.

Curie let her actions speak for her. Fingers flew across the keyboard.

"You're tracking the thief!" Nick said excitedly.

Using the satellite photos and information they had gathered before, Curie took a trip back through time. She spotted the first moment that the Masters' Motion Sensors went online in San Francisco, tracked the security detail that had been hired to monitor their safety, and continued right up to the day that Artemis had his sneezing fit around the corner from their home.

"There he is," said Curie. Sure enough, a man in a dark suit was seen crouching down in front of the planter.

"See if you can get a picture of his face," Nick said, totally excited.

Curie's fingers flew through a database of pictures until she found the right angle. A perfect picture of the culprit was on screen. She clicked "Save."

"Now what?" she wondered aloud.

Nick answered her question by turning the laptop toward him. It was his turn to be the bloodhound. Curie watched as her brother's fingers danced across the keyboard, bringing up programs and files. He found the one he wanted, and zeroed in on the missing Masters' Motion Sensor. It was in the parking lot. A few more taps on the keyboard brought up another satellite photo, but this one was in real time. Sitting in the passenger seat of one of the black sedans was the same man who was seen stealing the Masters' Motion Sensor.

"Yikes, I didn't know he'd be this close," said Nick.

They looked at the face of the man. There was nothing extraordinary about him. He was normal looking. He didn't look like a thief. But maybe that's why he was so good at it.

"It's hard to imagine that someone Dad trusted to protect his research tried to steal it," Curie said.

"We have to tell Dad," Nick said.

"Tell me what?" Both Nick and Curie looked up to see Artemis as he sat down in front of them, his nose red from blowing.

"Dad, it looks like the research has been tainted," Curie said.

"And to make matters worse, it was by someone you thought you could trust," added Nick.

"What are you talking about?" Artemis asked, pretty sure he didn't want to know the answer.

Nick and Curie broke down the bad news for their dad, detailing how they found the candy wrappers and other evidence along their journey. Nick thought he saw a smile cross his dad's face when they told him about how they used their brains and technology to uncover what was going on, but deep down he knew his dad was hurt.

"He was hired by the research company to make sure something like this wouldn't happen," Artemis said with a frown.

"I guess someone paid him more," Curie responded.

Artemis shook his head as he looked at the picture of the man he thought he could trust. "I guess there's only one thing left to do," he said. Artemis picked up his cell phone and dialed the police.

It wasn't long before police cars and television cameras filled the restaurant parking lot. Artemis stood nearby with his kids, sullen. This wasn't how he wanted things to end. They had learned that the

thief had stolen the Masters' Motion Sensor so it could be "reverse engineered," which meant someone would illegally take apart the device to see how it worked. Then they would try to make the device themselves, and make a profit off someone else's hard work.

Artemis let out a big sigh as the thief was placed into the back of the police car. Curie hung on to her father, then reached over and gave him a hug. He looked down at her, but his smile was pained. He then pulled Nick over as well, and hugged his children tight.

CHAPTER FIFTEEN:

IS THAT A RUMBLE, OR DID YOUR TUMMY GRUMBLE?

A sign read: *Welcome to New Madrid, Missouri.*

The town was peaceful, tranquil, and looked nothing like a town apparently in a direct line with disaster. The Masters of Disasters van was parked by the river alongside the black sedans and the men hired to watch over them. In the middle of a park, far from anything that could harm them in the event of an earthquake, Artemis, Curie and Nick set up their equipment.

"I don't know why we're doing this," Artemis said, his voice pained.

Welcome to New Madrid, Missouri

"Because we're Masters of Disaster, Dad, and we don't give up," Nick said proudly.

Artemis smiled, seemingly rejuvenated by his children's zest and belief in him. "You're right. We Masters never give up!" He fired up the equipment. "Let's see what we can do!" he shouted with newfound enthusiasm.

They all watched and waited expectantly for something to happen. But nothing came. No blips. No shaking of the ground. No warning signs. Time ticked away as they stared at the computer monitor. Their mood went from excitement to boredom.

"Maybe it's not connected correctly?" asked Curie.

Artemis looked at his watch. "No, we double and triple checked it. Everything is hooked up right," he said.

"Could it be sun spots? The Masters' Motion Sensors are sending the information by satellite," said Nick.

"There are no reports of solar showers," said Artemis. "We have to face the fact that we were tracking tainted data."

"Dad, one monitoring device being off the fault line is not going to adversely affect the others we laid down," said Nick.

"Oh, that's even better. My invention doesn't work!" Artemis barked.

"Dad, you know that predicting an earthquake is not like saying when the sun will come up," said Curie.

"I know that, but this is my life," Artemis said, sadly. "Every waking moment has been spent creating an early warning device for earthquakes. I feel like such a failure," he said as he hung his head.

"Was Thomas Edison a failure?" asked Curie.

Artemis' eyebrow raised, then his eyes, and finally his head. He looked at Curie, who had a huge smile on her face. She believed in him, and so did Nick.

"No, he was one of the greatest inventors the world has ever known," said Artemis.

"Okay, and what did Edison say when asked why he failed so many times before inventing the light bulb?" asked Nick.

Artemis smiled at his kids. He knew where they were going. "He said he didn't fail, he just figured out a thousand ways not to invent the light bulb," he said. "But I still feel like I let you kids down," he added.

"No you didn't, Dad. You taught us more about earthquakes, and how to prepare for them," said Nick.

"Yeah, Dad. You didn't fail, you just figured out one way not to measure earthquakes!" said Curie.

Artemis smiled, and then pulled his kids in for a hug. "Thanks, guys! Well, I guess we have 999 more tries at this!" said Artemis. He hugged them even closer.

"Who wants a milkshake?" Artemis asked. "There's this great little place just around the corner."

"What about the equipment?" asked Nick.

Artemis looked over his shoulder at the black sedans parked nearby. "There are five guys over there I think I can trust to watch it," he said as he waved to the men.

Curie and Nick held hands with their dad as they walked toward the malt shop, happy to be with him. *As they disappeared around the corner, the screen on the Masters' Motion Sensor computer* suddenly came to life. On the digital Richter Scale, the tiniest amount of movement had begun to register!

THE END

ABOUT THE AUTHOR

 Carole Marsh is an author and publisher who has written many works of fiction and non-fiction for young readers. She travels throughout the United States and around the world to research her books. In 1979 Carole Marsh was named Communicator of the Year for her corporate communications work with major national and international corporations.

Marsh is the founder and CEO of Gallopade International, established in 1979. Today, Gallopade International is widely recognized as a leading source of educational materials for every state and many countries. Marsh and Gallopade were recipients of the 2004 Teachers' Choice Award. Marsh has written more than 50 Carole Marsh Mysteries™. In 2007, she was named Georgia Author of the Year. Years ago, her children, Michele and Michael, were the original characters in her mystery books. Today, they continue the Carole Marsh Books tradition by working at Gallopade. By adding grandchildren Grant and Christina as new mystery characters, she has continued the tradition for a third generation.

Ms. Marsh welcomes correspondence from her readers. You can e-mail her at fanclub@gallopade.com, visit carolemarshmysteries.com, or write to her in care of Gallopade International, P.O. Box 2779, Peachtree City, Georgia, 30269 USA.

BOOK CLUB
TALK ABOUT IT!

1. In the motel room, Nick and Curie were both scared but had to be strong and calm for the sake of the other. When was a time you were scared but had to be really brave?

2. What are several things you can do to prepare for an earthquake?

3. Why do you think more earthquakes happen in the western parts of the country?

4. Why would someone want to steal a scientist's invention?

5. What's the scariest weather event you have ever experienced?

6. Do you think an invention that can predict earthquakes like the one Artemis Masters hoped to create is a possibility?

7. Who was your favorite character in the book? Why did you like that person?

BOOK CLUB
BRING IT TO LIFE!

1. Make an Earthquake Survival Kit! You learned about things that you might need in this mystery. Collect the proper items and get a secure box or container for them. Be sure to mark your box properly and put it in a safe place.

2. The earthquake ride at Universal Studios was both scary and exciting for the Masters kids because it was so realistic! Would you like to experience the earthquake ride? Think of some additions to the earthquake ride and share them with the group.

3. Take a piece of construction paper and tear it in two uneven pieces. Slowly slide the two pieces of paper back together. Do not try to fit the pieces together like a puzzle, just get close enough to doing so that the pieces of paper push up against each other or overlap. This is a great illustration of how the shifting of tectonic plates can form valleys and mountains after earthquakes!

EARTHSHAKING EARTHQUAKE TRIVIA

1. The Pacific Coast is the United States' most active earthquake zone. Florida and North Dakota have the least number of earthquakes, and Alaska has the most.

2. More than 8,000 earthquakes happen every day, but most are not strong enough to be noticed. That's about five or six every minute!

3. In 1811, an earthquake in Missouri knocked over chimneys 370 miles away in Cincinnati.

4. A really big earthquake can release 10,000 times the energy of the first atomic bomb.

5. Earthquake waves are measured by very sensitive instruments called seismographs.

6. Depending on the region, an earthquake can be caused by tectonic plate movement, volcanic activity, or explosions.

EARTHSHAKING EARTHQUAKE TRIVIA

7. Earthquakes under the ocean can cause huge waves called tsunamis.

8. The Richter magnitude scale was developed in 1935 and measures ground motion caused by an earthquake.

9. The largest earthquake ever recorded was a 9.5 on the moment magnitude scale. It occurred in 1960 along the Pacific coast of Chile.

10. "Moonquakes" are earthquakes on the moon, but they are smaller and less frequent than the ones on Earth.

11. Earthquakes can happen in any weather.

12. The most deadly earthquake in recorded history was in China in 1556. It killed about 830,000 people who were living in caves carved out of soft rock.

GLOSSARY

abort: to bring to an end before completion

aftershock: a small earthquake or tremor that follows a major earthquake

cleaved: clinged closely to

deliberate (adj.): carefully weighed or considered; slow, studied, and intentional

euphoric: exaggerated feeling of well-being

fault line: intersection of a crack in the earth with another surface

gloat: to have great or excessive satisfaction; often smug or malicious

impending: about to happen

languid: lacking in vigor or vitality; slow or slacking

lunar: of or pertaining to the moon

perilous: involving risk or hazard

GLOSSARY

Richter scale: the scale of measurement for determining the intensity of an earthquake devised by seismologist Charles Frances Richter in 1938; the Richter scale measures intensity on a scale of 1-10 with each increase of 1 indicating a 10-fold increase in energy

seismic: a way to describe something caused by an earthquake

TECH CONNECTS

Hey, Kids!
Visit www.carolemarshmysteries.com to:

Join the Carole Marsh Mysteries Fan Club!

Write one sensational sentence using all five SAT
words in the glossary!

Download an Earthshaking Word Search!

Take a Pop Quiz!

Download a Scavenger Hunt!

Get Earthshaking Earthquake Trivia!